Maisie goes to Hollywood

Maisie goes
to Hollywood

Author and Illustrator Aileen Paterson

THE AMAISING PUBLISHING HOUSE LTD

This story is dedicated to
Davena Turvey and Donald Douglas.
Have A Nice Day

Thank you to Anne-Marie Duffin (for signing Maisie's passport form) and to Nicholas Mathers of Glasgow.

© Aileen Paterson

Published in 1994 by
The Amaising Publishing House Ltd.
P.O. Box
Musselburgh
EH21 7UJ
Scotland

Telephone 031-665 8237

Printed and Bound by Scotprint Ltd, Musselburgh

Designed by Mark Blackadder

Image of KING KONG is through permission of Turner Entertainment Co.
Original copyright is in the name of RKO.

Reprint Code   10   9   8   7   6   5   4   3   2

It is the publisher's policy to use paper manufactured from suitable forests.

Other Maisie Titles in the Series:

Maisie and the Space Invader

Masie and the Posties

Masie's Festival Adventure

Maisie goes to School

Maisie goes to Hospital

Maisie Loves Paris

What Maisie did Next

Maisie in the Rainforest

Maisie and the Puffer

Maisie Digs Up the Past

Like many Scottish kittens, Maisie Mackenzie has relatives in far-flung places like Australia, Canada and America. This year she and Granny flew to California to visit the Hollywood branch of the family. It all began with a letter from Aunty Betty and Uncle Al inviting them over for a holiday. Granny was tickled PINK and Maisie was tickled to BITS, but when Mrs McKitty, their pernickety panloaf neighbour, heard Granny's news, she wasn't tickled at all!

"*HOLLYWOOD!* You would be far better coming to Skye with Miss Gingersnapp and me. Maisie needs fresh air and exercise. Just look at her, *glued* to the television set. She's got square eyes from watching all those silly films . . . and where are they made? Hollywood, of course!"

Maisie didn't hear a word. She was too busy watching her favourite filmstar, Honey-Pie Hotshot, wrestling with a cat-eating crocodile.

Granny tapped her on the shoulder and broke the spell.

"Wake up, Maisie. Mrs McKitty's right. All this television is turning you into a couch potato."

"A COUCH POTATO! What's that?" asked Maisie.

"A Tattie-on-a-Settee," laughed Granny. "Switch off that nonsense and let's go for a walk round the park."

Of course it was quite a different matter when Mrs McKitty and Granny wanted to watch *their* favourite films from Hollywood. They preferred the OLD films they'd seen when they were young and went to the cinema four times a week. When they were shown on television, Maisie, Granny and Mrs McKitty sat on the settee, like a ROW of wee tatties, munching pandrops and toffee eclairs. (Except when it was a scarey film, of course. Then Billy, the budgie, hid under his wing . . . and Maisie hid *behind* the settee!)

There were
Gangster Movies . . .
Badcats in Hats . . .
"Behaving like
absolute hooligans,"
said Mrs McKitty
. . . Musicals with
Tapdancing Cats
and Foxtrotting
Cats . . .
Ripping Yarns
about Fencing
Cats with
Trusty
Swords . . .

. . . and Cowboy Cats chasing mice in the canyons . . . Tarzan Cats yodelling up in the jungle trees . . . Daft Cats doing Daft Things . . . and Granny's favourites . . . handsome, lovey-dovey Cats.

Maisie loved these old films too. While Granny bustled about packing suitcases, she daydreamed about them, and imagined herself starring in one.

At last the day arrived for them to begin their American trip. Mrs McKitty and Billy the budgie saw them off at the airport.

"Tootaloothenoo," squawked Billy. "Send me a postcard for my cage."

"Cheerie-bye dears," cried Mrs McKitty, wiping a tear from her eye at the idea of Granny and Maisie travelling so far from Morningside, the very heart of civilization.

"California here we come," purred Maisie, as the big jet plane soared up into the grey Scottish sky . . .

The sky was brilliant blue over Los Angeles Airport when the plane came into land. Poor Granny's legs felt a bit shoogly after such a long flight, but when they stepped out into the sunshine, she soon forgot that. There, waiting to greet them, were Aunty Betty and Uncle Al.

They were the biggest cats Maisie had ever seen, and swept her and Granny clean off their paws when they gave them welcoming cuddles.

"It's really swell to see you both," beamed Aunty Betty.

"Hi there Haggis Bashers! Welcome to the United States," cried Uncle Al, picking up the luggage, and leading them out to the car park.

"Goodness me," said Maisie, "look at that huge lorry over there. It's a beauty!"

"That's no lorry, Maisie," said her uncle, "that's my *truck*. Hop aboard folks and let's hit the road for home."

In no time they were heading down the freeway with hundreds of other cars and trucks, whizzing past huge skyscrapers and tall palm trees on their way to Hollywood.

It was a great relief to Granny that her Californian cousins didn't live at the top of one of the skyscrapers, amongst all that traffic. When Uncle Al stopped his truck, she looked out and saw a bonny bungalow with a porch and, something to swank about to Mrs McKitty, a garden with a sitooterie and a SWIMMING POOL.

Hollywood is far from Scotland, and Maisie and Granny discovered that it was very different. The sun shone every day, for a start. American money was funny . . . dollars and cents instead of pounds and pence . . . and everything seemed to have a different name. Pavements were called sidewalks, and biscuits were called cookies, and petrol was called gas. Maisie discovered that American cats couldn't spell for toffee. They

wrote NITE for night, and DONUTS for doughnuts. What would her teacher, Miss Purrvis, say if Maisie did that!

The days went by. While Granny sat by the pool blethering to Aunty Betty, Uncle Al taught Maisie how to play Baseball. It was just like Rounders, so she soon learned how to whack the ball with her baseball bat. Then she taught Uncle Al how to play football. He was so huge that he filled up the space between the goalposts.

They all went out one night to a restaurant, and Maisie ordered a burger and an ice cream. When the waitress brought her order she soon saw how Uncle Al got to be so big. There was so much she couldn't eat it all, so the waitress put the rest in a doggy bag, in case she got hungry before bedtime!

Maisie at the Bat!

Uncle Al and Aunty Betty ate TWO giant burgers each, followed by Maple Walnut ice cream and coffee. *It didn't make them puffed-out though.* When they got home, they danced ROCK and ROLL to the music from their jukebox.

Maisie and Granny went shopping, and Granny said it wasn't a bit like going for the messages at home. They bought presents for everyone . . . T-shirts for Archie, Effie and Flora . . . tiny sunglasses for Billy . . . a hat for Mrs McKitty's collection . . . and a flowery shirt for Daddy. They sent them all postcards too.

Dear Effie,
Ho... you?
miss flora

Dear Flora
I'm having a lovely time in Hollywood. My Aunty... swimming... She has... pink car... big as a lorry— Lo...

Dear Mrs McKitty,
This is my best writing. America is hot. Granny has bought a pair of shorts, but they are long shorts, she says. Love...

Dear Billy,
Tweet-Tweet!
I've got you wee sunglasses, all well,
Love
maisie
x x x

Mrs marjorie mckitty
...side Mansion...
...urgh

Billy Budgie
care of
Mrs Mcki...
13, Mor...
Edinb...
SCOTL...

Dear Archie,
I've been teaching Uncle Al how to play football, and he shaved me how to play baseball with a big stick. Aunty Bet... makes Brownies and pecan pie— nearly as nice as millionaire... shortbread. Love...
from Maisie x
x

Dear Daddy,
Hello from Hollywood.
The sun shines every day, and America is full of cars and things to eat. You get funny breakfasts.—like pancakes and syrup, and you get chilli for your tea, but it isn't chilly. It's very HOT. I'm going to be in a movie!! I'll tell you all about it soon— LOVE and PURRS, Maisie x

Love
Maisie x

2, Haddock Place
Edinburgh EH10
SCOTLAND

Sandy
Mackenzie
P.O. BOX
2929 Ice
nr. Alaska.

One afternoon they all went for a stroll down Hollywood Boulevard, where the pavement is covered in gold stars with the names of famous film stars on them. Maisie was thrilled to find one with her favourite's name . . . Honey-Pie Hotshot . . . the bravest kitten in the movies. There was a Chinese Theatre with filmstars' *pawprints* in the cement courtyard outside. It was all very exciting for the two Scottish film fans.

Something even more exciting happened when they got back home . . .

Next door, in a big white house, lived Rufus T Walnutt the famous film director. He had seen Maisie in the garden playing football and baseball, and noticed how good she was. Mr Walnutt had a problem with his new film which was holding everything up. He was sitting on his porch worrying about it all when Uncle Al drew up in his truck, and Maisie jumped down. Mr Walnutt jumped up! He'd had a brainwave. This little tabby kitten from Scotland could be the very kitten to solve his problem. He ran next door to find out . . .

Uncle Al introduced him to his visitors, then Mr Walnutt explained why he had come to see Maisie.

His STUNT CAT, who did all the running, jumping and messy scenes instead of the star of his film, had fallen off his

skateboard. He had a broken leg! This meant that the last bit of the film, a chase through a swamp, could not be finished. He needed a kitten who was fit and fearless, and who looked *just* like the real filmstar . . . and Maisie fitted the bill.

"Would you be interested in doing some film work in the new Honey-Pie Hotshot movie?" he asked.

"HONEY-PIE HOTSHOT!! I would love to Mr Walnutt," meowed a delighted Maisie, "but why doesn't she do it herself? She's so brave."

Rufus T laughed.

"Why Maisie, a big star like Honey-Pie never gets her paws messed up. You won't catch *her* running through a swamp."

This was quite a surprise to Maisie. She got a few more

surprises when she arrived at the film studios next morning. Just after she got there, a big car driven by a chauffeur arrived bringing the famous Honey-Pie.

Maisie could hardly believe her eyes when Mr Walnutt introduced her to her favourite filmstar. She and Honey-Pie were just like twins! The only difference was that Maisie was smiling and holding out her paw, and Honey-Pie's face was tripping her. She wouldn't speak to Maisie. She just swept past and sat down on a chair with a star on it.

It was surprising to find that Honey-Pie was not as brave as she was cracked up to be, and now it seemed that she wasn't very friendly either.

Maisie's next surprise was a bit of a shock. She met the other star of the movie. His name was Elmer and he was a

DINOSAUR!

A big green scaly dinosaur!!! Maisie felt very uncomfortable. Honey-Pie sat beside her, not saying a word, while Elmer filled the silence making a terrible racket practising his fearsome roars. The ground was shaking!!

It was very alarming. You see, it was Elmer who was going to chase her through the swamp . . .

"Isn't it a wee bit dangerous to use a REAL dinosaur?" gulped poor Maisie.

Mr Walnutt patted her paw. "Don't worry about a thing, Maisie. Elmer is a sweetie. He's a CALIFORNIAN dinosaur, you see. He's cool . . . he hangs loose . . . and he's a vegetarian!"

Maisie didn't understand all of this, but she had read a lot about dinosaurs. The sight of Elmer's red eyes, and his huge sharp teeth and claws, made her very nervous. He didn't look much like a vegetarian to her. He looked awfully like a TYRANNOSAURUS REX!!!!

"OK. Let's start shooting," called Rufus T.

Honey-Pie stayed behind, but everyone else moved down to the swamp which had been made on the set. A half mile of smelly mud, surrounded by trees and jungly plants. Maisie watched while Elmer was filmed crashing about amongst the trees, thrashing his tail and roaring about how hungry he was . . . ! Then it was her turn . . .

Mr Walnutt explained to Maisie that he wanted her to run from one end of the swamp to the other pretending to be Honey-Pie, while Elmer tried to catch her.

"Ready Maisie. Now, try to look scared. Take One!"

Off she went, blundering through the squelchy mire, finding it very easy to look scared to death. Elmer gave a ferocious roar, and set off after her. Closer and closer he came, this hungry dinosaur, his teeth gleaming and his big feet pounding like thunder . . . chasing a bite-sized kitten! Maisie ran on and on, feeling Elmer's hot breath blowing her fur.

Suddenly disaster struck. Her paws got entangled in a low branch and she fell face down in the mud! She heard Elmer come running up, she saw his big green feet standing right beside her, and then she held her breath as he bent down and opened his mouth.

"Hi Maisie," he roared, "nice work. You deserve a bite. Would you like one of my beanburgers?"

Maisie sighed with relief as she and Elmer munched. It was nice to know a *nice* Tyrannosaurus Rex, she thought. The only trouble was that Mr Walnutt made them do the chase again . . . seven times!! Every time she got fished out of the mud for another 'take', she saw Honey-Pie laughing. It was very annoying.

Still, Maisie had saved the film, and Mr Walnutt was very pleased with her. He gave a party afterwards to celebrate the end of filming. That's when Maisie got her chance to teach Honey-Pie a lesson.

An orchestra was playing, everyone was dressed in their best for the party. There were lots of long tables covered with delicious food. Elmer headed for the salads, but Honey-Pie and Maisie were more interested in the ice creams and custard pies. Just as Honey-Pie reached out for a helping, a passing waiter bumped into her and the custard pie on his tray poured all over her. Everyone gasped! Big stars like Honey-Pie never get covered in sticky custard! She flew into a rage and began

hurling pies everywhere! There was another gasp, but nobody dared to move. One of the pies had sploshed all over Maisie, but *Maisie* didn't fly into a rage. Instead, she looked round at the custardy cats and laughed! Then she picked up a pie and flung it right at Honey-Pie! Next minute every one was hurling pies at one another! Thwack! Plop! Splosh! You never saw such a mess in all your life! The pies were fairly whizzing through the air and landing on faces, fur and whiskers . . . and the funny thing was that every one was laughing. There is nothing so funny as a custard pie fight! When the last pie was gone Maisie collapsed on the grass and turned to find Honey-Pie beside her, tired and sticky but smiling.

"I'm really sorry I was so mean to you, Maisie," said Honey-Pie. "I guess I got too big for my boots, being a big Hollywood star. It was great fun getting all messy and being like an ordinary kitten. I hope we can be good friends now."

Maisie smiled back and said yes, and then she and Elmer and Honey-Pie washed off the custard and the party began all over again.

Maisie's holiday in Hollywood was nearly over. It was time to repack the suitcases and say Goodbye to all her new friends, and to Aunty Betty and Uncle Al. Granny was beginning to get homesick for Edinburgh and mince and tatties, and the wind and rain. Maisie had had a lovely time, and her daydream had come true, but now she was looking forward to seeing Morningside again and giving everyone their presents. She wondered how Billy would look in his Californian sunglasses.

There was a big surprise for them both at Edinburgh Airport. Daddy was waiting to welcome them back to Scotland and give them lots of cuddles.

Maisie's presents were a great success. Billy looked a picture in his Californian outfit. Daddy said his flowery shirt fitted purrfectly. Archie, Effie and Flora couldn't *wait* to try on their American T-shirts, and Mrs McKitty loved her new hat. She said it would be the talk of Jenners' tearoom!

When *'Honey-Pie Fights Back'* opened in Edinburgh, Maisie and her friends all got invited to a night out at the Morningside Cinema. They all clapped when the chase through the swamp was on! When the film finished, and the credits rolled up showing the names of everyone in the film, the audience cheered. There, at the very end, they saw Maisie's name . . .

"With lots of love and thanks to our special Stunt Cat, Miss Maisie Mackenzie of Edinburgh, from Honey-Pie, Elmer, and Rufus T Walnutt."

Glossary

panloaf	an affected way of talking
pernickety	fussy
couch potato	someone who sits for hours watching television
pandrops	peppermint sweets
shoogly	shaky
bahooky	bottom or hips
blethering	chatting
swell	wonderful
parking lot	car park
freeway	American motorway
swank	boast
sitooterie	patio
doggy bag	popular American idea – what you can't eat goes in a bag to take home
messages	shopping
brainwave	sudden good idea
'face was tripping her'	she was sulking
cracked up	said to be
cool	unflappable
'hangs loose'	is easy going
racket	noise

—See you all soon,
love maisie x